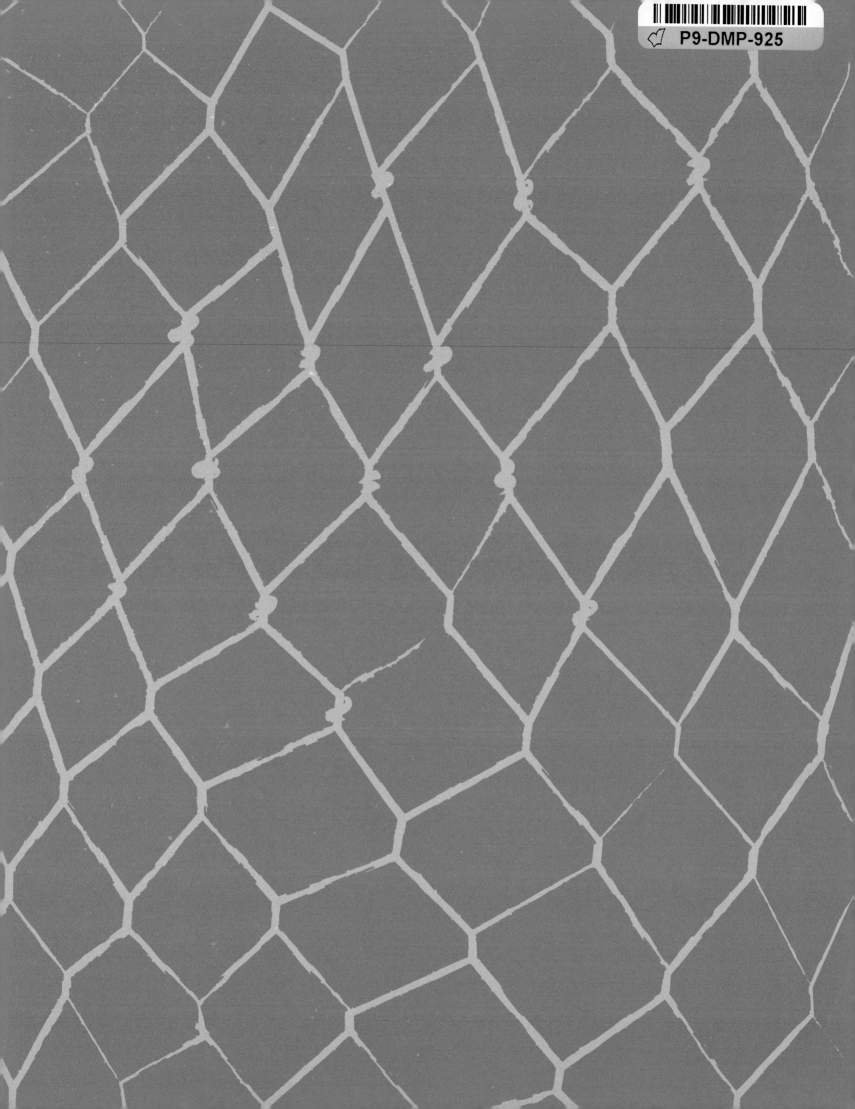

SHARKY McSHARK

For Matthew, Riley,
Rudi, and Max
XOXO
AM

· Little, Brown and Company · Hachette Book Group · 1290 Avenue of the Americas, New York, NY 10104 · Visit us at LBYR.com · Originally published in 2020 by Orchard Books, an imprint of Hachette Children's Group, in the United Kingdom as Sharky McShark and the Teensy Wee Crab · First U.S. Edition: June 2021 · Little, Brown and Company is a division of Hachette Book Group, Inc. · The Little, Brown name and logo are trademarks of Hachette Book Group, Inc. · The publisher is not responsible for websites (or their content) that are not owned by the publisher. · Library of Congress Cataloging-in-Publication Data · Names: Murray, Alison (illustrator), author, illustrator. · Title: Sharky McShark / Alison Murray. · Other titles: Sharky McShark and the teensy wee crab · Description: First edition. | New York; Boston: Little, Brown and Company, 2021. | "Originally published in 2020 by Orchard Books, an imprint of Hachette Children's Group, in the United Kingdom as Sharky McShark and the Teensy Wee Crab." | Audience: Ages 4–8. | Summary: Sharky is the meanest, most fearsome creature in the deep until an accidental encounter with a tiny crab shows her a better way in this tale reminiscent of "The Lion and the Mouse." · Identifiers: LCCN 2020028610 | ISBN 9780316706872 · Subjects: CYAC: Bullying-Fiction. | Sharks-Fiction. | Crabs-Fiction. | Friendship-Fiction. · Classification: LCC PZ7.M95674 Sh 2021 | DDC [E]-dc23 · LC record available at https://lccn.loc.gov/2020028610 · ISBN 978-0-316-70687-2 · PRINTED IN CHINA · APS · 10 9 8 7 6 5 4 3 2 1

SHARKY McSHARK

Alison Murray

LB

Little, Brown and Company
New York   Boston

Down at the bottom of
the deep, blue sea lived the
meanest, most **fearSome**
creature that had ever swum
in the watery depths.
Sharky McShark
was her name.

and even the rocks
got out of her way.

Aha—Sharky always eats
her CRUST-aceans!

Sharky was the biggest bully
in the sea. She had no friends,
and she didn't want any.

Being a lone shark was best,
she thought to herself.
I don't need a sole.

Being a lone shark was best,
Then, one day, out of nowhere . . .

PLONK!

. . . a teensy-wee
crab bounced off
Sharky's fin, nipped her
nose, and landed on the
seabed in front of her.

"Who dares nip
my nose?"
said Sharky McShark.
"I will eat
you right up."

Oops!

Sorry!

The teensy-wee crab quivered with fear.
"Please don't eat me!"
she cried. "Spare my life and I promise
I'll return the favor. You never know
when YOU might need MY help."

Well, Sharky McShark found that VERY funny. "Help?" she sneered. "From a teensy-wee thing like YOU?!"

HA HA!

Sharky laughed . . .

HAHAHAHAHA HA!

and laughed

and laughed.

HA HA HA HA

HA HA!

She laughed SO hard
that she tumbled backward
into an old fishing net . . .

that was tangled
on the hook of a
rusty anchor . . .

that was attached to an
ancient wreck . . .

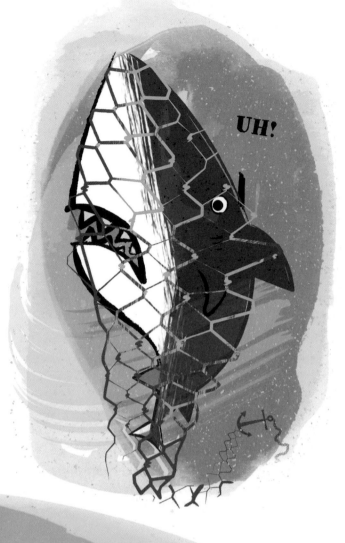

that was balanced
on the edge
of a
deep-sea abyss.

For the first time
in a hundred years,
the old ship
creaked . . .

Oh dear!

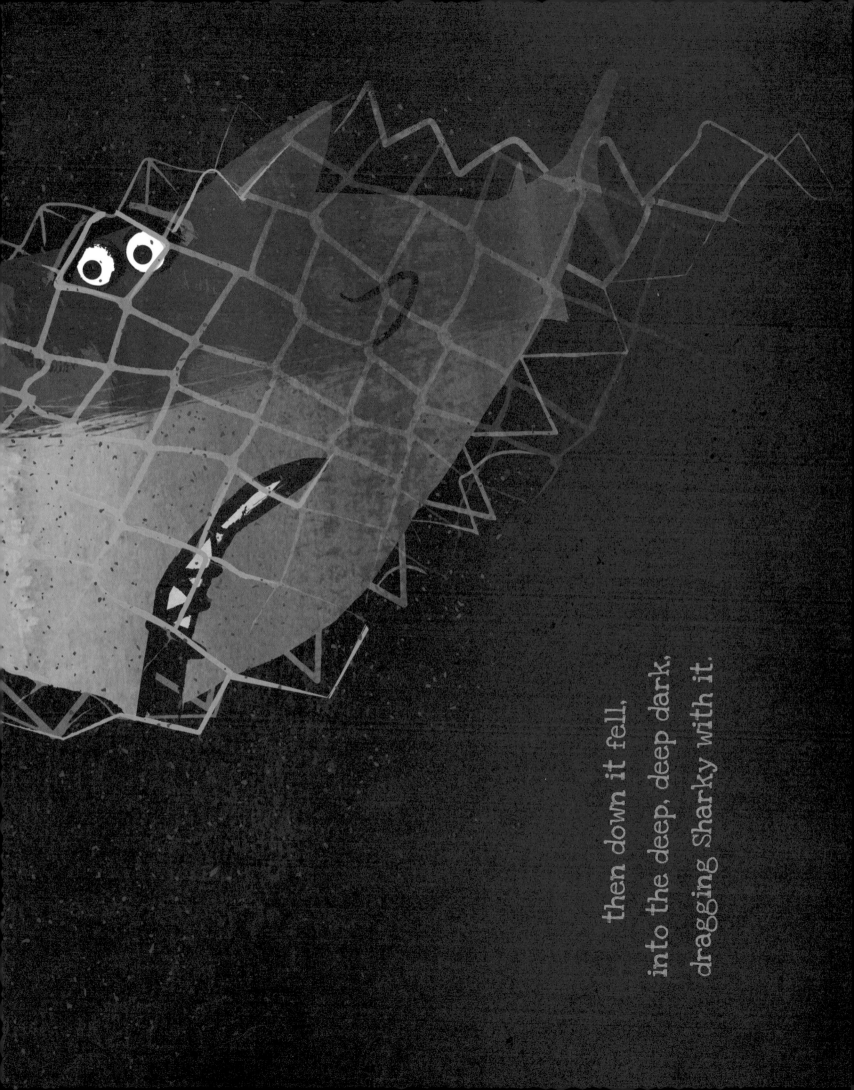

then down it fell,
into the deep, deep dark,
dragging Sharky with it.

Lying
at
the
bottom
of the
deep,
dark abyss,
Sharky
McShark
was
no longer
the
meanest . . . .

or the most
fearsome creature
in the sea. . . .

She was the loneliest.

"I wish someone would come to
my rescue," said Sharky McShark.
"I wish I had ... a friend."

In her heart, Sharky realized
that making a new friend
meant taking a chance—a *scary* chance.

"I'm a bully because I'm afraid . . .

afraid that no one will like me."

And now it's too late,
thought Sharky.

Then, all of a sudden, out of nowhere . . .

PLINK! PLANK! PLONK!
Someone familiar bounced off
Sharky's nose and landed
on the seabed in
front of her.

The teensy-wee
crab set about
snipping and snapping,
clipping and cutting,
until at last . . .

Sharky was free!

And right then and there, she decided to do the biggest, bravest thing she had ever done. . . .

"Will you be my friend?"

She asked.

"Of course!" said the teensy-wee crab, who knew that even big, bad bullies deserved a second chance.

And as it turned out . . .

Thank you for helping me!

Sharky McShark
was no longer
the meanest,
most fearsome
creature in the
deep, blue sea. . . .

She was the **friendliest.**